Baby, It's Cold Outside

Baby, It's Cold Outside

USA TODAY BESTSELLING AUTHOR
MELANIE HARLOW

NEW YORK TIMES BESTSELLING AUTHOR
CORINNE MICHAELS

Copyright © 2019 by Melanie Harlow and Corinne Michaels.

ISBN Print: 978-1-7323718-2-8

All rights reserved.

No part of this book may be reproduced in any form or by any electronic or mechanical means, including information storage and retrieval systems, without written permission from the author, except for the use of brief quotations in a book review.

Cover: Sarah Sentz, Enchanting Romance Designs

Editing: Nancy Smay, Evident Ink

Preface

Dear Reader,

A long, long time ago, two baby authors became friends. We bonded over knowing nothing, cried when things did poorly, and cheered when the other was doing well.

Years later, those two authors decided to co-write. It was a complete chance that the friendship would remain intact or the book would be written. It did. It was called Hold You Close. After that we wrote Imperfect Match.

Our careers have continued without co-writing anymore, but we had a little fun with a holiday story. Baby, it's Cold Outside is a really fun, cute, Christmas story where we are totally goofy and lean into the silliness.

Even still, it's one of the best experiences we had (or at least Corinne will say that).

We hope that you enjoy our festive story and love Harlow and Michael as much as we do.

This novella does connect with Imperfect Match so if you haven't read that book, we highly recommend it. It's also adorable (again, according to Corinne where Melanie forbid her to kill anything or anyone.)

One

HARLOW

"Ugh!" I scream as I try to pull the damn tree through the glass doorway of my new apartment building—unsuccessfully. I've been at it for ten minutes and even in the freezing cold December-in-Chicago weather, I have sweat beading on my forehead. What the hell was I thinking trying to move a six-foot-tall live tree by myself?

Oh, I know, I was listening to Willow talk about how a tree with lights would be magically jolly for my psyche, and necessary to get out of the foul mood and bad luck I'm enduring. Pfft. I should've known better. Willow may be the best boss and top matchmaker in Chicago, but she was wrong on this.

I don't feel jolly. I don't feel festive. I feel sweaty and frustrated, and I would like to shove this tree right up Santa's ...

I give it another yank and my hand scrapes against the bark, ripping a hole in my glove.

That's it. I'm over it all.

"Stupid Christmas and all its stupid holiday crap. Santa ... blah! Who needs him and his jolly elves when life sucks? Stupid tree, stupid holiday, and stupid joy!" I kick the stump, then wince because it hurt.

"Well, that's not very festive," a deep voice says from behind me. "I don't think the tree did anything to deserve your hatred."

Of course someone is standing here, watching me like a freaking idiot. What a sight I must be too. I'm holding the cut end of a tree, trying to drag it through the heavy door that keeps closing, ripping off branches as I pull harder. I'm not sure whether I should laugh or cry.

I huff, my hair falling into my face, obstructing my view of my current life crisis. "Sorry, I'll apologize to it later." I don't even turn to look at the stranger because *whatever* with it all anyway. "Once I get it in the stupid door."

I'm a damn mess, but what else is new?

Two weeks ago, I got dumped. Merry-fucking-Christmas to me. Instead of the gorgeous ring I was hoping for, I got the gift of finding out my boyfriend of six years wanted to ride someone else's sleigh. So I packed my shit and left. Thankfully, my boss had just moved in with her fiancé, so she gave me the keys to her fully furnished apartment and told me to add plants because plants cure everything.

I should've gotten a bunch of fake ones—that way I wouldn't kill them—but Willow insisted I get a real Christmas tree to push myself into the holiday spirit.

And even in the absolute craptastic state I'm in, I wanted to fake it till I made it. I'm vying for partner of My Heart's Desire and every little thing helps, right? I should've known better. Now I'm going to have a big half-alive, half-naked tree to look at, one more reminder of how I'm failing at life.

Well, if I can get it upstairs.

I pull on the tree again, tug-of-war style, needles flying everywhere. I debate just leaving it here. There's no tree in the lobby, so I can just call it a contribution, right? If it was my name on the lease, and not Willow's, I might do it. Or maybe if I didn't care about my job or had another place to live, but alas, I don't. So the tree must go to its final resting place where it will undoubtedly die before the big fat guy makes his way on the 25th.

"Are you planning to put that in your apartment?"

"Yup," I say as I yank again. It doesn't budge. "Well, maybe."

He lets out a chuckle. "Need help?"

"Nope," I say through gritted teeth. "I got it." I wipe my brow where the sweat is now dripping and groan aloud. "I'm fine. It's fine. I got this."

"You know I can't leave until you get this tree inside."

I can hear the smile in his voice. At least I'm amusing him.

"I'm happy to help since you're struggling."

This is the worst week of my life.

The voice behind me sighs loudly. Giving in, I turn to ask for the help I so clearly need, ready to deal with the embarrassment of my life.

"I'm not strugg—" I start, but when I turn, I want to die. Because in front of me is the most attractive man on the planet, standing there with a smile on his face.

He has dark brown hair that's pushed to the side, but not in that slick way—it's as though it just moved there because he commanded it to. His jaw is strong and covered with a dusting of stubble that I want to brush my fingers against. And then there are his eyes. Jesus Christ. His eyes are the most stunning shade of blue. They're not quite royal blue, although I could see specks of it. They're a deep, rich sapphire color with traces of green, or is it just a lighter blue? Either way, I can't stop looking at him.

My mouth hangs open just a bit as I try to get my brain to form words. What do you say to a god?

"I can see you're not, but ... I'm a gentleman, it's Christmas, and you know ... I have somewhere to go before New Years."

"What?" I ask, not remembering if there was a question or whether I am supposed to do something besides stare at him like the present I'd like under my tree.

"Are you ready for me to help?"

Yes, the answer is yes. Yes to anything he wants. Yes!

"Huh?" is what comes out past my lips.

"The tree. Are you going to let me help you?" He grins at me, knowing my only other choice is to leave it here, stuck in the doors.

"Help?"

"*Yeeeeah*," the word comes out slowly, which is apparently the cylinder I'm firing on. He puts his coffee cup down and then extends his hand. "I'm Michael."

What a name. It's simple, classic, and so totally him. I think there was an angel named Michael, right? Maybe a god? If not, there is now. The god of Sexy Men. That is Michael.

I sigh, my eyes blinking slowly as I stare at him.

His head tilts just a little, lips pursed as he waits expectantly.

Shit. I should talk. "Harlow."

"Harlow?"

"Yes?"

He smirks. "Your name is Harlow?"

If the ground could just open me up and swallow me, that would be cool. "Sorry," I say as I take his hand like I should've to start with. "Yes, I'm Harlow, and this is my tree that is resisting its new home." I'm hoping I can recover from this horrific introduction with a modicum of self-respect intact.

"I hear that some trees are just difficult."

"This is apparently the story of my life."

Men. Trees. People. Parents. They're all difficult. What's that saying about the common denominator? I'm starting to wonder ...

"Well, let's see if we can't get the tree upstairs and willing to behave."

"Doubtful, but I appreciate it."

Michael moves to the double doors and pushes one to the side and then slides in a locking mechanism I didn't know existed, and then repeats it on the other side.

Seriously, I hate my life. "That *would've* made it easier ...."

He gives me a panty-melting smile and his brows rise. "And probably saved a lot of branches."

"That too."

"Why don't you grab the top?" he suggests.

I move to the front of the tree, resisting the urge to punch myself in the face.

"Ready?"

I nod.

With almost no effort, we move the tree through the doors and to the elevator. "Thank you, I can get it upstairs."

Michael gives me a look that says he's not so sure of

it, which I've earned. "I'll help you get it to the apartment. You know, there are two more doors to get it through."

I laugh, because what the hell else can I do? "I'm never going to recover from this. This is the most embarrassing thing ever."

"I'm sure I have you beat."

"Really?"

He shrugs. "Have you ever been to Cancun for spring break?"

I've never gone anywhere outside of Chicago. "Can't say that I have."

"Then I promise, you're not even in my wheelhouse of embarrassing moments."

I appreciate his attempt to make me feel better, but this definitely blows. If he wasn't so attractive, maybe I wouldn't care, or if he wasn't a guy, it would be fine. However, he is both and I am mortified.

I push the button to go to the twentieth floor and will myself not to say anything stupid on the elevator ride up.

"So, are you new to the building?" Michael asks.

"Yeah, just moved in about a week ago. It was my boss's old apartment, but since she and her fiancé just bought a townhouse, she's subletting it to me. You?"

"I've been here about a year. I live with a buddy from college."

"I used to live with my boyfriend, but I don't now.

Nope. Now I'm alone. *Totally* alone. And single." I'm also wondering if I can sew my mouth shut to stop myself from blurting out stupid stuff.

Michael gives me a smile and runs his fingers through his hair. "Well, that's ..."

"A lot of info?"

He laughs.

"I swear, I have my shit together most days, but it's been a rough week."

"Well, the holidays are either great or total shit, right?"

"I'm definitely on the shit end."

His eyes roam over my body and his lips turn up as my blood heats under his stare. "Here's to hoping today shows you it's not all shit, then. Maybe we can turn your luck around."

He stands there, holding the trunk of the tree and then the elevator door opens, not allowing me to think any more on that statement.

Two

MICHAEL

Do not stare at her ass. Do not stare at her ass. I try to tear my gaze away, but ... it's really fucking hard to do with those leggings she's got on.

It's been a long time since I've had a reaction to a woman like this. I could've stood in that hallway all damn night watching her. She's beautiful in an imperfect kind of way. Her long brown hair is falling out of her ponytail, and there are a good amount of pine needles stuck in there too, but it just makes her more adorable. Not to mention how the tip of her nose is just a little bit red from the cold. I can't remember the last time I found someone's flaws so cute.

We get the tree into the apartment without any issues. "Do you have the tree stand?" I ask.

"The what?"

"The stand ... that the tree goes in."

"You mean, it doesn't just ... stand on its own?"

I can't tell if she's kidding, and I fight back laughter because the look in her eyes says she's not and she's halfway to tears.

"Not a big deal," I say quickly. "It can sit in the corner while we go get a stand." I don't know what possessed me to say it. I don't know this girl and she doesn't know me, but I'll do anything to not have her cry.

"Right now?"

I look down at my watch and then back at her. Fuck the family party I'm supposed to be at. I didn't want to go anyway, and I'd much rather help someone who is clearly having a bad day. My sister will understand, and if not, she can kiss my ass.

I smile at Harlow. "Yeah, we'll go to the store, and then I'll help you set it all up."

Her eyes brim with unshed tears and now I wonder if I fucked up by offering to help. "You'd do that? You don't ... I mean, you're all dressed up. Don't you have somewhere to go?"

I lift my shoulder, not really thinking much of it. "I think helping a neighbor is the Christmas spirit thing to do, don't you? Besides, if you don't get it in the stand with water, who the hell is going to help you get it out of here when it's dead?"

The sound of her laughter goes straight to my cock. It's soft but lacks all restraint, and I find that I want to hear it again.

"I probably would just toss it out the window," she tells me.

"And that is why we're getting a stand now."

"Can you give me a few?"

I nod. "I'll wait here."

Harlow rushes out of the room and I look around at the apartment. Knowing she just moved in a week ago, I'm shocked at how organized it is. There aren't any boxes, unlike in my place, where my buddy and I have lived in for two years and still haven't finished unpacking. Everything in here is neat and clean. There are a few photos on the table where she tossed her keys, and I wander over to them.

I pick up a framed picture of an older couple, assuming it's her parents. Harlow looks exactly like the woman in the photo, only younger. A guy I'm guessing is her brother is in a cap and gown next to her.

Ugh. Northwestern.

"Hey, where did you go to college?" I yell out.

It's best to get the important things out of the way.

"Me? Oh, I went to U of I!"

Okay, so it's just her brother that is the enemy.

Setting that frame down, I move to the next photo, where Harlow stands next to another woman in an office. The other woman's arms are wrapped around Harlow's middle and the smile is so wide, it could break the glass. Who the hell has photos in their house with their boss? They must really get along.

"Hey. Sorry," she says quickly as she comes up behind me. "Find anything interesting?"

I laugh because it's clear I was doing what any normal person would when left alone in a stranger's house. "Nope. Seems you're normal."

"Sorry to disappoint."

"Is that your boss?"

Harlow nods quickly. "That's Willow. She's my boss-slash-friend. She owns the company I work for, but I'm going to come on as a partner soon. Well, if I'm able to match this client who is totally a pain in my ass."

"Match?"

She bites her lower lip. "Yeah. So. I'm a matchmaker."

"Like..."

"Like exactly what you're probably thinking, yes. I hate the term and really wish we could come up with something a little less cheesy. Like, Destinymaker or Couple Counselor. I don't know, I'm still mulling it over, but the point is that I cut through the crap and find what people want in a partner."

"I think you found your new job title—crap cutter."

Harlow rolls her eyes with a grin. "I'll be sure to float it to management. It's super romantic."

"I'm a romantic guy."

She tilts her head. "Are you? Interesting."

I groan, seeing the wheels start to turn in her matchmaker brain. The last thing I need is another woman in my life trying to set me up. My mother and sister are bad enough. "Actually, no. I'm not romantic at all. I hate romance."

"You and me both, buddy."

"Wait a minute. You make your living as a matchmaker, and you hate romance? Isn't that sort of a detriment to your career?"

She sighs and blows the stray pieces of hair out of her face. I notice she's put on lipstick. Her cheeks look a little brighter too, and she's put cover-up or something on her nose, but it's still pink. "I suppose it is. I haven't always hated romance. It's more of a recent occurrence."

"I see. That boyfriend you mentioned ..."

"Ex-boyfriend," she says sharply.

"Right. Ex-boyfriend. Is he responsible for your hatred of romance?"

"Probably." She crosses her arms over her chest, not easy to do since she's still wearing her puffy winter jacket, and her lower lip juts out. It's angry and adorable all at once. "I thought he was going to propose on Christmas Eve, but he dumped me right after Thanksgiving. After everything I did for him, he dumped me!"

"What did you do for him?" I ask, curious.

"Oh, God." She shakes her head. "I was so dumb. I

loaned him money to get out of debt, because I thought he was going to buy a ring. Instead, he bought two tickets to Maui and took his little side dish on Christmas vacation! Mele fucking Kalikimaka!"

"Ouch. How long were you together?"

"Six years."

"Six years!" The thought of a six-year relationship—seventy-two months, over two thousand days and nights of unrealistic expectations—nearly makes my knees buckle. "Damn."

"I was an idiot. But I kept thinking he loved me and eventually he'd want to marry me."

"Why'd you want to marry him?"

She thinks for a second. "He was cute enough. And he had a steady job. However, he also had a gambling habit I didn't know about."

"Got it." I look around. "So if I open drawers in here, will I find a little voodoo doll with a Hawaiian shirt on?"

Her brown eyes light up. "That is a great idea."

I laughed. "Why don't we stick to the tree stand for now, huh? I'll run out to the store. Where do you want your tree to go?"

She drops her arms and turns in a slow circle. "Maybe over there by the window?"

"Good choice." I check my watch. If I hurry, I can go buy her a tree stand, set it up by the window, and make it to my sister's party by nine, ten at the latest.

"Okay, I'll be right back."

"Wait! I'm coming with you."

"You don't have to. It's freezing out there. Why don't you stay in and get warm?"

"I am warm."

"Oh yeah?" Unable to resist, I reach out and touch her nose. It's still chilly. "Doesn't feel that way."

She sighs. "My nose always gets so red from the cold. I hate it."

"I think it's cute."

"Cute like Rudolph?" She eyes me warily. "That's what my ex used to call me."

"Let me just say right now that your ex was a real big asshole who didn't deserve you, okay? And I don't care what he looked like or how steady his job was. Even if he kicked the gambling habit, he was never going to deserve you."

"But you just met me," she says softly. "How do you know that?"

"I just do." And the urge to kiss her at that moment is so overwhelming that I have to take a step back. Like she said, I just met her. I don't want to be that guy. "Come on. Let's go."

❄

We walk the three blocks to the drugstore with an icy Chicago wind blowing in our faces, the cascading flurries growing thicker. I'm not sure how much snow we're going to get this evening, but it could make for a long ride out to my sister's house in the suburbs.

"Can we slow down a little?" Harlow asks, her shorter legs scrambling to keep up with my long ones. "I'm dying here."

"Oh, sorry." I shorten my strides and move a little less briskly. "I was trying to hurry because the weather's getting worse. I have a long drive tonight."

"I knew it!" She whacks me on the arm. "I knew you had somewhere to be. You should have told me. I can handle this myself."

"Harlow, you were never going to get that tree up to your apartment if I hadn't intervened. And even if you did, what was your plan—decorate it lying down?"

"I told you, I hadn't really thought that far ahead. I don't know anything about Christmas trees! We had an artificial one growing up. It stood on its own. Why shouldn't a real one?"

"Oh my God. Come on in here." I put my arm around her to shepherd her through the revolving door to the store, and it feels so good I wish I had a reason to keep it there.

"They have tree stands here?" Harlow looks around. Her nose is bright red again, and I want to warm it up with my lips. What the hell is wrong with me? I don't even know this girl's last name. And other than putting makeup on, she hasn't really given me any indication she's interested in messing around tonight.

Tearing my eyes from her face, I look for the holiday aisles. "Over there," I tell her. "Aisles eight and nine."

Three

HARLOW

We make our way toward the other side of the store, and I grab an abandoned shopping cart along the way. "I might need some other things too."

"Like what?"

"Like decorations. Lights and ornaments."

He glances at me. "You don't even have lights or ornaments?"

"No, and stop making me feel bad. Getting the tree wasn't even my idea, it was my boss's."

"What did you do last Christmas?" he asks.

My spirits sink even lower as I remember. "I put up a tree with the asshole ex in our apartment, but it was fake, just like his love for me. And I don't want any of the stupid ornaments that we hung on our fake tree with our fake joy in our fake happiness. It was all a lie."

"Oh, Jesus." Michael sighs heavily.

"I'm going to grab some vodka too. Be right back." I veer off down aisle four and head for the booze section. They probably won't have my favorite brand here, but beggars can't be choosers, and I really need something to take the edge off this holiday angst.

Too bad Michael won't be able to stick around long enough to have a drink with me. It sounds like he has to drive somewhere, and the weather is getting worse by the minute. I'm lucky we ran into each other and he had mercy on me—I'd probably be stringing lights on a tree still stuck in the lobby door if he hadn't.

God, he's so damn cute. And charming. And sweet. There was a moment in my apartment, right after he touched my nose, that I thought he was going to kiss me, but he didn't. Did I imagine it?

Duh, of course you imagined it, you dummy! All you've done is make an ass of yourself and talk about your ex. He probably looks at you and thinks crazy ex-girlfriend. And look at the way he's dressed—that man is too hot to be alone on a Friday night. He's got a date.

I pull a bottle of vodka off the shelf and place it in my cart. Then I add a bag of Hershey Kisses, a box of candy canes, and a tube of ready-made sugar cookie dough. In aisle eight, I grab a few strands of lights and a box of colorful ornaments. Since we're on foot, I don't want to buy too much, but I can't resist picking out a star for the top.

I find Michael in aisle nine looking at a box in his

hands. My stomach flip-flops a little as I approach. He's so tall. I wonder what he looks like underneath all those clothes, and for a moment I fantasize about unwrapping him layer by layer. The winter coat and scarf. The suit and tie. The buttoned-up shirt. I wonder if it has French cuffs or not.

I love French cuffs.

He catches me staring at his hands, which are strong but elegant-looking, with long fingers. "Do I need a manicure or something?"

Embarrassed, I feel my face get hot. "No! Sorry, I was just wondering something."

One of his eyebrows cocks up. "About my hands?"

Oh, dear God. "Uh, about your shirt actually. Whether or not it has French cuffs."

"Why were you wondering about my shirt?"

Because I was thinking about taking it off of you is not an appropriate answer, although I'm almost tempted to give it. I mean, why not—I've been spewing every thought in my head without a filter all night long, haven't I?

But in the end, I don't.

"I guess I just like a nice dress shirt with French cuffs."

He looks amused. "And why's that?"

I shrug, figuring I might as well be honest. "I think they're classy and convey there's something powerful about a man. But it's an understated kind of power. Like he might drive a Range Rover and drink expensive scotch, but he'll still pull your hair and say dirty things to you."

He doesn't say anything for a moment, but his eyes stay locked on mine. The tension between us ratchets up about a hundred notches. "Yes."

I'm so lost in the heat of his gaze that I forget the question. "Yes, what?"

"Yes, my shirt has French cuffs." He places the boxed tree stand he's holding in my cart. "Yes, I drive a Range Rover." Then moves closer to me, so close I can feel his breath on my lips. "Yes, I drink expensive scotch."

I can barely breathe. My throat is dry. "And the other stuff?"

He smiles the slightly sinister grin of a well-heeled villain. "Come on. I have to let *some* things come as a surprise."

While I'm standing there, equal parts turned-on and dumbfounded, he takes the cart from me and pushes it toward the front of the store.

Jolly Old St. Nicholas! Is this guy for real?

I feel like I might look for him again only to find he's been nothing but a figment of my imagination. Do guys like Michael exist outside of fantasies and romance novels? Is he secretly a serial killer? Am I going to wind up tied up in my closet tonight?

Actually, the idea has some possibilities ...

It takes me a couple minutes to recover my senses,

and by the time I find him near the registers, he's already paying for all my loot. "What are you doing?" I ask, frantically tugging on his sleeve. "You don't have to buy all this!"

"Harlow, it's not that big a deal." He pulls out a credit card from his wallet, but before he can swipe it through the reader, I grab it.

Michael West.

"Hey, that's funny," I say.

"What is? You stealing my Amex?"

"No. Your last name is West. Mine's North. North ... West ... we have the same kind of last name." I don't know why it makes me so happy, but it does. We're both directions! We're both witches from Oz! Together we're Kim Kardashian's baby! It has to be a sign, right?

"Nice to meet you, Harlow North." He quickly snatches the card out of my hand and swipes it. "Now quit being a pain. I've got this."

I huff and pout, but there's not much I can do since the transaction is complete within seconds. "Thank you. It was really nice of you to help me at all, let alone pay for my drunk tree-trimming party supplies."

He laughs and gathers up three of the four bags, including the bulky one holding the tree stand box. "Is that what all this is?"

I grab the last remaining bag, which contains my

candy and cookie dough. Maybe I'd just eat it right from the tube. "Pretty much."

We exit the store and immediately, a frigid blast of air hits us. The snow is coming down hard and heavy now, and it's tough to see even five feet ahead. The ground is slippery too, and I slide a little as we make our way down the sidewalk.

"Careful." He switches all his bags to one hand so he can take my arm. His touch sets off a spark that warms my entire body. I swear every snowflake that lands on me sizzles.

"So where are you headed tonight?" I ask, hoping it sounds like an innocent question.

"To my sister's in Lake Bluff." He looks up and down the avenue. "But the drive is going to be so fucking slow."

"Do you have to go?" Inside, I'm shrieking for Christmas joy that he's not going on a date. Visions of sugarplums and his naked body dance in my head.

"I should. It's my family's Christmas party, and I skipped it last year."

I nod, focusing on the sidewalk again as my sexy visions go poof and vanish. Unless ... "You know, your sister probably wouldn't want you on the road in this blizzard."

"Oh no?"

"Definitely not. In fact," I tell him as we reach our

building, "I think you might want to call her and tell her not to expect you."

"Really." He sounds amused as we make our way to the elevator.

"Of course!" I punch the button. "I mean, no pressure or anything, but I know I wouldn't want my brother on the road tonight."

The elevator doors open. It's empty.

"Ah. Very sweet of you." He lets me enter first, then hits twenty.

"It's just too dangerous," I insist as the doors close. "You could get in trouble out there."

He leans back against the wall and looks over at me, his expression smoldering. "I could get in trouble right here."

Four

MICHAEL

What the hell am I doing flirting with this girl (who is clearly going through a breakup) instead of being with my family (who are going to kill me for this) and wondering if her tree isn't the only thing we're going to get erect tonight?

I never think like this. I'm a logical guy who makes logical choices. I don't walk girls to get tree stands in the middle of a blizzard, no matter how red their noses get.

"You know, they say that decorating a tree is not something you should do alone," Harlow says as we reach her door.

"Who says?"

"Everyone."

"Is that so?"

She nods. "It's the Christmas law. I heard about it

on the internet and you know that everything you read there is true."

"I would hate the break the Christmas law."

Harlow's brown eyes sparkle as if I just gave her the best present in the world. "Really?"

"Under one condition ..."

"Name it."

She agreed to that way too quickly. My mind wanders a bit before I remember what I wanted to say. "We don't mention your shitty ex one more time tonight."

She extends her hand, and I take it. "You got yourself a deal."

We enter the apartment, tree still standing in the corner, thank God, and get to work. Harlow puts some cheesy Hallmark movie on the television and then brings in a mug of hot chocolate. "Here, it's also law that we have to drink this."

"This is a law I don't mind." I have a feeling her laws are only going to get more numerous as the night wears on, but I have a few laws I hope to enact as well. I'm such a dick. I have to stop my mind from going down this road each time she looks at me.

But she's so damn cute. When we got back, she put on a pair of way-too-fucking-short shorts, a tank top (as if it's not ten degrees and snowing right now), and tortoise shell glasses. She's got that hot-for-teacher vibe going on right now and I'm dying.

I take a sip and it's hot, but it's not hot chocolate. "What the hell is in this?" I ask.

"Whipped Vodka, you don't need the whip cream when you have it in alcohol flavor."

"You know, drinking and tree trimming is probably a bad idea."

She smiles. "Are you worried that you'll get into trouble, Michael?"

"I'm worried *you're* what's going to be trouble."

"Well, I've been on the nice list for a long time and it's gotten me here ... maybe trouble isn't so bad." Harlow bites her lower lip before bringing the mug up to her mouth. She takes a slow sip, watching me over the rim and my cock goes hard.

"Are you flirting with me?"

She sets the mug aside and sidles closer. "Maybe."

"I think you are and I think you want me to kiss you," I challenge her. I love when a woman is assertive and it's clear that Harlow is testing her boundaries. She's about to find out that there are some games I won't lose. Enjoying the surprised—and pleased—look on her face, I place my mug on the coffee table next to hers.

"And what if I do?" she teases.

I raise my gaze upward, and feel a sly grin form on my lips because right above her head is mistletoe. While I don't need the excuse, I'm happy to use it to my benefit. "Well, sweetheart, look up."

"Huh?" Harlow tilts her head back and I take that opportunity to grab her and pull her to my chest.

She lets out a squeak in surprise and her hands grip my arms. "What does the law say about mistletoe?" I ask.

Her tongue darts across her lips, and I don't wait for her reply, taking that as invitation enough, and I kiss her. She tastes of chocolate, vodka, and sweetness. I've never been so attracted to a woman this quickly, but Harlow is like a siren song, one I want to answer.

At first, the kiss is slow and tentative, but then she moans and all of that shatters. Her lips part and I delve into the heat of her mouth. She kisses me back just as rough. I love when a woman doesn't hold back. Her hands drift up to my neck, holding me to her.

I slide my palms beneath her tank and up her bare back. Her skin is soft and warm and—

CRASH!

Harlow squeals and we jump apart as the tree hits the floor.

"Damn that tree," she says breathlessly. "It's evil and it hates me."

I have to laugh at her indignant face. "It's just a tree. How could it be evil?"

She arches a brow. "Clearly you have never heard of a Whomping Willow."

"Can't say that I have."

"Don't tell me you haven't read Harry Potter."

"Why not?" I manage to right the tree and prop it in the corner again.

"Because then I won't know if we can become friends."

I give her a look over my shoulder. "Is that what we're doing tonight? Becoming friends?"

"Of course. What else would we be doing?" Harlow pushes her glasses up her nose and gives me her best innocent little lamb face, all the while standing there in those fucking tiny little shorts.

I'm not sure she's wearing a bra either. If she is, it isn't doing much to hide the fact that her nipples are hard. It's hell trying not to stare at her chest.

I slip out of my suit jacket, tossing it on the couch. "Well, my friend, why don't you help me get this tree in the stand? Maybe all it wants is a permanent home. Some nice decorations. A drink of water."

"I have to water the tree?"

"Yes, Harlow. You do." Shaking my head, I grab the box with the stand in it from the drugstore bag. "It's a good thing I'm here."

"I'll drink to that," she says, picking up her mug again and taking a sip. "Okay, tell me what to do to help."

We manage to get the tree into the stand, the bolts secured, and some water in the base. Harlow doesn't have a tree skirt, but she does have a red fleece blanket she drapes around the base of the tree, and once it's in place, she stands back and claps her hands. "I love it! Let's decorate!"

I glance out the window. The snow is falling even heavier now, and if I stay even one more minute, I will never make it to my sister's house. She'll make me pay too—my entire family will. Nobody can work a guilt trip like my mother, and my sister can hold onto a grudge like it's keeping her alive. They have the ability to make my life very unpleasant.

But when I look at Harlow again, she's standing on tiptoe to hang an ornament high up on the tree, her bare legs beckoning. My cock stirs again in my pants.

Yeah, fuck my family Christmas. There's something I want to unwrap right here.

"Hey, I need to make a phone call real quick," I tell her.

"No problem. You can use my room if you'd like privacy," she offers, pointing to a door off the living room.

"Thanks. I'll be right out." I head into her bedroom and shut the door behind me.

Curious, I take a moment to look around her room before I make the call. It's feminine and neat, no surprise there. Pink, black, and white bedding. A million decorative pillows perfectly placed. One nightstand stacked with books, the other holding only a lamp, which is on. I lower myself to a bench at the foot of her bed and call my sister.

"Hello?" She already sounds peeved.

"Hey, it's me."

"Let me guess—you're not coming."

"Laura, the weather's terrible! I can't drive in this."

"How convenient."

"Look, I wanted to come this year. I really did."

"It's like you *knew* I was planning to set you up tonight!"

"Set me up?" I frown. "With who?"

"I forget her name. She's a friend of Reid Fortino's fiancée."

"Who the fuck is Reid Fortino?"

"God, you don't remember anybody! He's a co-worker of mine, and you've met him at *least* five times."

"Oh. Well, thanks but no thanks. I don't need to be set up."

"Michael, you can't keep turning down every single girl I send your way!"

"Um, yes. I can, actually." In the living room, I can hear Harlow singing "Have Yourself a Merry Little Christmas," and it makes me smile because it's so off key.

"You're going to wind up old and alone."

"That's a chance I'm willing to take." I get up and open the door to peek at Harlow, stifling my laughter at the sight of her stringing Christmas lights around her body.

"Good Lord, what's that noise? Did you adopt a sickly cat?"

"No," I tell her, quickly shutting the door again. "It's a neighbor singing. I have to go."

Laura sighs dramatically. "What am I supposed to say to this girl if she shows up hoping to meet the man of her dreams?"

"Say Merry Christmas. Pass her the cheese plate."

"You're a big jerk," she huffs. "I'm giving your present to somebody else. And if that girl shows up and she's perfect, you'll be sorry you're not here."

"I'll take my chances," I tell her. "Bye, sis. Sorry to miss the party. Give my apologies to Mom and Dad, and I'll see you guys soon." I end the call and hurry out of the bedroom.

The perfect girl is already mine tonight.

Five

HARLOW

Michael shuts the door to my bedroom, leaving me alone in the living room. I can't help dancing around as I admire my tree and start hanging ornaments on its branches.

"I'm sorry I called you evil," I tell it softly. "You're the perfect tree, and I'm having the perfect night."

Opening up a box of lights, I wonder who Michael had to call. For a second, a wave of fear rushes through me as I imagine him calling his girlfriend—or wife!—making up some lame excuse why he's going to be home late. But before I panic completely, I remember that he said his sister is having a party tonight. He was probably calling her to say he can't make it because of the weather.

Scolding myself for assuming the worst, I sing along with the soundtrack to the holiday romance on the TV as I unwind the lights. Not everyone is a two-timing asshole like my ex, and I have to get over it and start trusting people again—like the hot, sexy man in a suit who rescued me this evening. The one in my *bedroom*.

"Have yourself a merry little Christmas," I croon loudly, even though I am a terrible singer and Willow says I really should not ever sing in public. "Let your heart be liiiiiiiiight." I loop a strand of lights around my waist and toss one end over my shoulder, twirling in circles. "From now on our troubles will be out of sight."

"Wow." Michael shuts the bedroom door behind him, his expression amused. "That's quite the vocal talent you have there."

I laugh. "I happen to have many talents. Singing, alas, is not one of them."

"I gathered that conclusion from the next room."

"Everything okay?" I glance at the phone in his hand as he walks towards me.

"Everything is great." He tosses the phone onto the couch next to his coat. "I am not expected anywhere else tonight."

"Perfect." I can't keep the smile off my face as I twirl around, showing off the lights I'm wearing. "I was just about to test these and make sure they work."

He puts his hands on my hips and pulls me closer. "Want me to try to turn you on?"

"Yes, please." I lift my lips to his and he kisses me, and I would not have been surprised if every damn bulb on the string lit up just from the current between us.

His mouth moves down my throat, sending sparks to the farthest reaches of my body. His hands slip beneath my tank top and slide up my sides. His breathing grows heavier as his palms move down the back of my shorts and grip my ass. He pulls me against him, and I can feel how hard he is. My belly hollows, and my core muscles clench.

I reach down between us and run my hand over the warm, hard length of him, and my legs go weak. Is it wrong that I want this near-stranger to fuck me senseless tonight?

"How am I doing?" he whispers, his breath warm on my neck. "Are you turned on yet?"

"Um, yes—and then some." I want to move into my bedroom, but I worry it might be too forward. Luckily, he's not nearly so concerned.

"Think the tree will mind if we give it some alone time?"

"Not at all," I reply, a little breathless. "Want to—"

But before I can finish my invitation, he scoops me up and carries me toward my room, throwing open the door and then laying me down across the foot of my bed. My heart pounds wildly as he closes the door, returns to the bed, and removes my glasses, setting them aside on the nightstand. I'm happy the lamp is on, so I can see him, but I'm still freaking out a little.

"I've never done this before," I blurt. "Brought someone into my bedroom the first night I met him."

"I've never done this before either," he says, holding up one end of the stand of lights wound around my body. "Removed Christmas tree lights from someone in bed."

"I'm a different kind of girl," I tell him, giggling as he unwinds the string and drops it to the floor.

He loosens the knot in his tie and stretches out above me. "I like that. I like everything about you, Harlow North."

"Even though I'm clueless about Christmas trees?"

"If you weren't, I wouldn't be here." He grabs my tank and lifts it over my head, revealing a red lace bra that is more decorative than anything else. His bright sapphire eyes pop. "And I'm *really* fucking glad to be here right now."

I smile as I wrap my legs around him. "Good."

We make out just like that for a good long while, and I can't believe how hot it is—the material of his dress shirt against my chest, the way his cock rubs against me through layers of clothing, the way I'm nearly naked but he's still wearing a fucking tie.

He moves his body over mine in a way that lets me know exactly how good it would feel if we got rid of all the barriers between us. I'm not exactly sure how far we're going to take this, but it's not long before he's got me panting and writhing beneath the weight of his body, frustrated by the need to get closer to him.

How bad would it be to have sex with a stranger? I

mean, is he still a stranger? I know his last name, right? And I know where—roughly—he lives. We're practically neighbors! And I know he's the kind of guy to rescue a damsel with a tree in distress on a snowy December night ...

Good enough for me.

Apparently he's feeling the same way, because just as I'm about to swallow my pride and reach for his belt, he picks up his head and says, "Hey, before this goes any farther, I just want you to know, you can tell me to stop at any time."

"Okay."

"So," he says, kissing his way down my chest, "do you want me to stop?"

"Not even one little bit."

He looks up at me, his mouth hooking into a smoldering crooked grin. "Good."

He takes his time.

I don't know whether he's worried he'll never see me again or really does just want to lavish every inch of my skin with attention, but he undresses me with an agonizing lack of haste—first my shorts, then the bra, then finally the matching panties, which make him groan when he sees them.

"Did you know what you were doing?" he demands, moving down so his head was between my legs. "Did you put these on knowing they'd drive me crazy?"

"Maybe," I tease.

"You are definitely on the naughty list," he tells me, and then his hands are pushing my thighs apart and his mouth is on me and I can feel his lips and tongue making me wet right through the lace. Eventually he drags them down my legs and tosses them aside, circling his tongue right over my clit until I'm so close to orgasm I could weep. He drives me to the brink of insanity, taking me right to the edge of a climax I'm desperate for, and then backs off again.

"Please," I whisper, clawing at my comforter.

"Please what? You have to ask for it."

"Please let me come."

"Do you think a naughty girl like you deserves it?" he asks, sliding two fingers inside me.

"Yes!" I cry out, both in pleasure and in answer to his question.

He laughs and gives me what I want with his mouth and his hand and tongue and I'm rocking my hips beneath him, shameless and needy and moaning so loud I'm positive the neighbors can hear me.

But I don't care—it's the best orgasm I've ever had.

When my body stops its rapturous pulsing, I push his head away and scoot back. "Stop, stop," I say, totally out of breath. "I can't take any more."

"Oh, but you will." Michael stands up and removes his cufflinks, and it's so fucking hot watching him, my toes curl. When he pulls out the knot in his tie, I bite my lip. He's just starting to unbutton his shirt when I hear a voice in the living room.

"Harlow? Where are you?"

Michael and I exchange a surprised look.

"Expecting company?" he asks, his hands paused.

"No!" I stage whisper. "It sounds like my boss, but I have no idea what she could be doing here!"

"How did she get in?"

"She must have kept a key. This used to be her place, remember?"

"Hey!" Willow knocks on my bedroom door. "You in there? Get dressed, we're going out!"

"Um, one second!" I scramble to find clothes as Michael laughs silently, shaking his head. "I'll be right out."

I manage to tug on underwear, my shorts and tank, and a robe that was hanging on the back of my door in about ten seconds. Putting a finger over my lips, I look at Michael, and he nods. Then I open the bedroom door just enough to slide out, pulling it shut right behind me.

Willow is standing in my living room, hands on her hips. "That's not what I had in mind for a festive holiday party outfit," she says. "Can you put something else on? And maybe brush your hair?"

I pat my bedhead hair and tighten the robe around me. "What festive holiday party?"

"It's a Christmas party hosted by Laura Thompson

from Reid's office, and it's always super fun. Plus, there's someone there who wants to meet you."

"Who?"

"A guy." Willow's expression is sly. "Laura Thompson's little brother. She showed me his photo last year and he's hot as hell. I know he'd be perfect for you. I don't need to remind you that I'm a spectacular matchmaker, do I?"

"No, but—"

"Then hurry up, we're already late. Reid's waiting for us in the lobby."

The last thing I want to do is leave my apartment to go meet someone's little brother at a Christmas party. "Thanks, but no thanks. I'm not feeling well."

"You're feeling fine, you're just depressed. Although nicely done on the Christmas tree." Willow gestures toward the spruce in the corner. "That's a step in the right direction."

"I'm not depressed, I swear. And you have to go now." Taking her by the shoulders, I spin her around and walk her toward the door. "Bye. Say hi to Reid. Have fun at the party."

Willow sighs as she steps into the hallway. "Fine. But if that super hot guy is there and asks about you, you'll be sorry you spent the entire night holed up in this apartment."

"Maybe."

"You can't just retreat, Harlow. You have to go after

love if you want to find it. You're not just going to look up and find it standing there."

It almost makes me burst out laughing. Maybe I hadn't found love tonight standing there in the lobby, but I had found a damn good time. "Night, Willow. I'll talk to you tomorrow. Drive carefully in this weather, okay?"

Before she can try to drag me out again, I shut the door in her face, put the chain on, and rush back into my bedroom.

I close the door, toss my robe aside and lean back against the wood. It feels extra cool because I'm still burning up from that orgasm. "Hi."

Michael smiles. "Hi. Everything okay?"

"Yeah, my boss was just ... it doesn't matter."

"Come here," Michael says crooking his finger at me.

Six

MICHAEL

While Harlow stepped out to deal with whomever it was that stopped by, I lay there trying to make sense of what the hell is happening.

How did this girl, whom I just met, manage to get me to break all of my rules? I never fuck on the first date. And I usually spend a good amount of time making sure I don't end up with a stage-five clinger.

Still, I can't seem to help myself.

"Kiss me," I demand.

And she does.

It takes me no time to get hard again. The second I saw those brown eyes after she closed the door, flushed and still glowing a little after she came on my tongue—it's all I need. She tastes like sugar and spice and everything fucking fantastic.

"You have too much on," Harlow says as she stands at the edge of the bed right between my legs.

"Yeah?"

"Definitely."

"Well, what are you going to do about it?"

She grins. "I'm thinking that *maybe* we should remove some of it."

"Just maybe?"

Her fingers move to the buttons of my dress shirt. She slowly pushes each one out of its hole, moving down lower and lower. I groan as she lets her nails scrape down my undershirt, loving the way her breath hitches when she feels the muscles beneath.

Harlow drops to her knees. "I need to be eye level," she murmurs, her voice thick with desire. I swear, I'm going to blow like a teen on prom night if she wraps that fuckable mouth around my cock.

I close my eyes for a second, thinking of anything unsexy to try to get a grip.

Spiders. Pizza. Elephants.

Then she makes a low moan and there's not a damn thing I can think of to reduce how fucking turned on I am.

"Promise me you're not crazy," I find myself saying, because this girl is pretty damn perfect. Not that I think crazy people realize they're nuts, but I'm praying she's not. My last girlfriend was a money-grubbing bitch. All she wanted was the family money and status.

It's why I've sworn off dating anyone who knows who the hell I am.

Michael West, heir to the West Investment millions.

She looks up through her sooty lashes. "I'm not. Promise me you're not an asshole who is going to treat me like a pariah tomorrow."

I take her chin in my hand, forcing her to look at me. "I promise."

"Good, then you're still overdressed and I'm very much wanting to get back where we were."

"Me too, baby."

Fuck, I'm calling her baby. And not in that condescending way that some dudes do. The way I say it is like all that happened tonight was what was meant to. Like some fucking Christmas miracle is happening and Santa brought me exactly what I asked for.

A beautiful girl with red bra and panties that I want to ride all night.

Harlow goes for the button of my pants and I stand. That right there is a sight. She's on her knees in front of me, the perfect height to take my cock right now.

And then she brings her face right there. She hooks her fingers in my pants, taking the boxer briefs down with her.

"Merry Christmas to me," she says with a look of awe.

Yeah, that's every man's fantasy right here. A girl

who looks just as turned on to suck my dick as she was when I was eating her out.

"I think we were both on the nice list," I say as I run my fingers through her hair.

"Let's find out."

Harlow doesn't hesitate. Her perfect lips wrap around my dick and she takes me deep. "Fuck." I let out a groan, head falling back as she sucks.

I've always been more of a giver when it comes to sex. I get turned on by the woman getting off, and I love nothing more than pushing her past her limits. Right now, though, it's really nice to receive. Her hot mouth is exactly where I want to be. Harlow's fingernails scrape against my thigh, sending a myriad of sensations through my body.

She bobs her head up and down, and then I slip my fingers in her silky brown hair. "Let me fuck your mouth."

Harlow moans and I take that as permission to do as I please. God, this is best fucking night.

I start to move my hips, her hands now gripping my ass. "You look so hot on your knees with my cock in your mouth."

She takes me even deeper and the surprise of it almost makes me lose it.

I jerk my hips back, not wanting to come too early and then I pull her up. "I want you."

"I want you too."

"We can stop now." I give her another out.

Harlow's big brown eyes are filled with desire. "No, no stopping."

Yes, Virginia, there really is a Santa Claus. The quote from *It's a Beautiful Life* springs into my head instantly.

I don't say a word as I lift her up and gently lay her down on the bed. She's so damn beautiful. It's funny that in just one night this girl has me all mixed up. I blew off my family party, carried a tree, and took her shopping, all just to see her smile.

I can't remember the last time I cared about something so simple.

She isn't here because I'm some rich guy who can afford to buy her entire apartment, let alone a tree stand. Sure she might not be able to sing worth a damn, and she doesn't know how to open a door properly or have even a basic knowledge of plant life, but she's kind. She cares about her friends and her job. And she has the most stunning smile I've ever seen.

Which she's giving me right now as I look down at her.

"Hi," she says.

"Hi."

"What are you thinking?"

"That your smile is beautiful," I answer honestly.

Her eyes soften and she touches her hand to my lips, moving her thumb. It does something to my heart.

"You have no idea how glad I am that you rescued me," she says softly.

That makes two of us. I'm hoping I can rescue her a lot more too. I want to wake up with her in my arms on Christmas morning and start a whole new tradition of holiday unwrapping. I want to bring her to my parents' house, introduce her to my annoying sister, and then ring in the New Year with a kiss at midnight.

Where the hell did this feeling come from? Jesus, I'm losing my damn mind.

I shift the conversation back to the sex. Sex is what she wants. Sex is what we both want. I don't need to think beyond it. "Because you're about to have some earth-shattering sex?"

"No, that's just a bonus."

"Condom?" I say, trying to keep myself distracted. Because I can't possibly be falling for her. No, it's the snow. The cold has somehow frozen my brain. That's all.

She reaches over to the nightstand. "I'm really hoping Willow left some condoms." Harlow digs around in the drawer and then screams with delight. "I found some! Oh, we have a whole strip."

I take it from her hand, ripping the wrapper open with my teeth and roll it on.

"Here, let me help," she says as her hand slides down my dick, unrolling the condom as she goes.

Not wanting to wait another second, I take her

wrists in my one hand and pin them over her head. Then I surge inside her with raw force.

"Oh! Oh God!" she moans and I give her a second to grow accustomed to my size.

After another second and feeling the way her pussy grips me, I start to move. I hold her down, thrusting inside her over and over. Her eyes close and she moans again. I move my free hand down between us and rub her clit.

I'm so fucking close.

I want her to come again, this time around my dick.

"Harlow," I urge her. "Come, baby. Come again."

Her eyes close and she takes her lower lip between her teeth. "I'm going to come," she moans and I increase pressure on her clit.

I feel her tighten. "Yes, that's it, Harlow, let go."

And she does.

I thrust harder, chasing my own release, which comes in record time. The feel of her pussy milking me is too much. I surrender to it, taking the last moment of bliss, and work to catch my breath.

That was ... whoa.

After a few seconds I lift my head to look at her. Her hair is spread out on her pillow, her lips are swollen, and a lazy smile plays on her face.

Her eyes open and she lets out a soft chuckle. "If that's being on the naughty list, I'm never coming off."

I laugh and rub my nose against hers. "Are you okay?"

"I'm glorious. I'm pretty sure I heard angels sing on that last one."

"Me too."

"Glory be to God and all that."

"Pretty sure God wasn't with us, but I'm open to you thinking I'm close to being one," I tease.

"You earned it."

I kiss her once and then reluctantly get off the bed. When I glance back at her, she's now clutching a pillow and curling herself up. Her ex is a goddamn fool, and I'm very happy he is.

Seven

HARLOW

B est. Sex. Ever.
      Like, ever, ever.

People write songs about the sex we just had and they aren't sad ones. Jesus, who knew I could have multiples?

I want to scream into the pillow but manage to pull myself together. I told him I wasn't crazy, and that might give him some doubts. But this day has been a whirlwind and I'm not really sure how to process it all.

First, I had mind-blowing sex. That in itself is worth screaming about.

Second, I really freaking like him. Michael is fun and even though he's a little naughty, sometimes it's good to balance the goodness I tend to lean toward. I'm always the good girl, doing what people ask, finding them love, blah, blah. Maybe putting my tiara away and grabbing the broomstick will be a change that leads to more fun.

And by fun I mean multiples.

Third, I am not a one-night-stand girl, and this is a problem.

My sexual conquests always have meaning, and I at least know the guy a little, but I don't know Michael at all. But he's sweet, he can put a tree up, and he must have at least some feelings toward me, right?

Do I ask him to stay?

Do I see if he wants to go for another round?

I don't know the rules in this situation, and that's something I'm not used to.

All of these are first-world problems, but it's the world I live in.

I chew on my thumbnail as I mull it all over and try to think logically. If Michael wants to leave, he can—it's not like he has to drive. And if this is all we ever have, I can be a mature adult. Not to mention, this isn't my forever apartment, so if it gets super awkward, I'll just move.

It's not that serious. It's just a night.

One incredible, unforgettable night.

"You okay?" he asks, and I jump a little.

The pillow is covering my bare breasts, and again, I'm faced with not knowing where to go with this. "Uhh, yeah, I just need to ... use the bathroom."

He smiles, his naked body on full display and it takes

every ounce of my restraint not to stare at his cock. I really like it. It did magical things, and I'd like to see if it was just a fluke or not.

I mentally slap myself. I promised not to be crazy and I will uphold my end of the bargain.

I do my business and walk back out. When I enter the bedroom, Michael is on the bed, covers up to his waist, but his chest is bare. God, he is a work of art.

"Come here," he says with his arms open.

And I go without pause.

"I know you said you never do that ..."

I look up. "I don't. I'm a serial monogamist. Not really by choice, but I typically only sleep with guys I really like, and never on day one."

"It's not really my normal, either. I usually at least know more than just some basic information."

That makes me feel marginally better. "What do you want to know?"

"Family?"

"My parents are still happily married, for over forty years now. I have one brother who isn't married, and I swear never will be. Even though I've tried to match him at least three times."

"So your matchmaking skills are a questionable thing."

I sit up with narrowed eyes. "I'm the best in this city."

He grins. "Good to know."

I sense challenge in his voice so I don't let it go. "Seriously! I have more marriages than Willow, who owns the company, and her sister, combined. I'm like a *super* matchmaker."

"One who doesn't believe in romance?"

I sigh and pull the blanket up to cover my chest. "Okay, if we're talking about *me*, that's different. In my experience, romance is fleeting. It comes and goes and people claim they're always searching for it. But it's not something you find, it's something you work for. I want love. I want a guy who looks at me twenty years down the road and thinks I'm cute with my hair turning gray and my wrinkly face. Romance is this ..." I lean down and kiss him, "... feeling in your chest."

His hand comes up, tangling in my hair, and then he pulls me back to his mouth. He kisses me reverently and I feel it in my toes. "Romance isn't bad."

"No," I agree. "It's not, but love makes your heart race and it is a simmer that doesn't ever fully go out."

Our eyes stay on each other's. My chest is tight as we both are silent, but I feel like he's saying something anyway. Before I can search too deep, he releases me. I sink back against his chest, not wanting to think about what that was.

Michael clears his throat. "Okay, so brother, work, and parents are covered. What else should I know?"

"Hmm." I use this time to compose myself. "I'm a

Scorpio, I like horribly cheesy Christmas movies, I love guys who rescue girls with trees."

His laughter vibrates against my skin. "I like girls who need rescuing."

"Ahh, so you're a Romeo type?"

"I'm not sure I'm a type at all."

"Everyone is a type," I tell him.

Then I sit up and study him. Now that my libido is a little in check, I look at Michael as I would a client. How would I match him? Maybe this is the approach I should take on dating. Leave the emotions and that lusty goodness out and start to be analytical, the way I would if I were helping a client.

This thought has merit.

"Why do you look like you're about to dissect me?"

I grin. "Would you let me try?" And then I realize that he probably isn't thinking the same meaning as I am. "I mean, let me look at you not just as the guy who gave me not one but two fantastic orgasms, but as a potential match for someone."

"I'm going to regret this."

"Probably, but it'll be fun."

"You know, you're the second woman today who has tried to set me up." Michael shakes his head.

"Really?"

"Yeah, my sister, Laura—that's whose house I was supposed to be at—said there was some girl coming that was"—he air quotes—"just perfect."

"No way!" I laugh. "Willow, who, err, interrupted us earlier, was trying to do the same. She wanted to drag me to some work party of her fiancé, Reid."

Michael looks at me a little funny, like he just smelled something weird. "Reid? You said—you said Willow's fiancé is named Reid?"

"Yes." I cock my head to one side, recalling something he mentioned a moment ago. "And did you say your sister's name is Laura?"

"Yeah."

Chills sweep down my arms, although I'm not cold. "Is your ..." I clear my throat, thinking back to what Willow said. "Is your sister's last name Thompson, by any chance?"

"It is." Michael swallows and sits up a little straighter in bed. "Is this Reid guy's last name something Italian?"

"Fortino," I whisper. We stare at each other, our eyes going wide. I almost expect the music from the Twilight Zone to start playing.

"Oh my God." Michael blinks, leaning back against the headboard. "I don't fucking believe it."

"Me neither." It can't be ... can it?

"Are you thinking what I'm thinking?" he asks.

"That we were both supposed to be at the same party tonight so that we could be set up ... with each other?" Even as I speak the words, it strikes me as too coincidental. Too unbelievable. Too insane.

Michael shakes his head. "It's fucking crazy. But I think it's true. My sister works with Reid. And she said his fiancée was bringing a friend who'd be perfect for me."

I start to laugh. I can't help it—this entire night has been so ridiculous and fun. "And Willow said I had to go to this party tonight to meet the little brother of this Laura woman who works with Reid."

"Christ." Michael runs a hand through his hair.

"I guess we saved them the trouble," I wheeze. "Who'd have thought?"

"Right?" Michael laughs too, a deep, joyful sound that warms my insides. "I can't believe it. My sister was right about something." He pulls me onto his lap so I straddle his legs.

"They're all going to flip out," I tell him. "Willow especially. She'll try to take credit somehow."

He wraps his arms around my waist. "So will my sister. But I didn't need them to find a perfect girl. I found her all on my own."

I grin. "Stuck in a doorway with a Christmas tree. God, it sounds like a Hallmark Channel holiday movie, doesn't it? We had our very own meet cute!"

"Do Hallmark Channel movies have sex in them?"

"Not onscreen." I giggle. "It's more like behind closed doors."

"Your door is closed." He flips me onto my back and

covers my body with his. "And I'm very interested in a happy ending right now."

"Me too." We kiss, and I wonder if I'll ever get enough of his sexy mouth on mine.

I wonder if this is the start of something as good as it feels. I wonder if someday we'll be telling our meet cute story to our children and grandchildren—maybe it will be the one we tell every single Christmas as we put up the tree. And I wonder if it's possible to fall for someone so fast, because as he moves inside me again, I feel myself spinning head over heels. I never want it to end.

Of course, I don't *say* that to him.

But later, as we're saying goodbye at my door, I tell him that tonight feels like an unexpected gift.

"For me too," he says. He kisses my forehead. "And I, for one, would like to open it again tomorrow night. And maybe even the night after that."

"Really?" My toes tingle, and I can't keep my smile from getting bigger.

"Really. I don't know what you did to me tonight, Harlow North, but I'm under your spell. And I'd like to stay there for a while."

I lift my shoulders. "You know where to find me."

And he does—the next night, and the next night, and the next. In fact, we don't spend a night apart for the following year and a half, and two years to the day after he came to my rescue in the lobby, I walk down the aisle and become his wife.

We celebrate our first Christmas as Mr. and Mrs. West in our own home, where Michael is in charge of getting the tree in the stand, I am allowed to bake but not sing, and we laugh about how destiny wanted us together so badly, it left us no room to mess up.

Christmas miracle? Maybe.

But one thing is for sure—we were always meant to be.

THE END

We hope you enjoyed this fun Christmas story set in the Imperfect Match world!

If you loved this story, be sure to check out Imperfect Match which is FREE in Kindle Unlimited! There is a special sneak peek on the next page to give you a glimpse of Reid and Willow!

PART ONE
Imperfect Match

Rule number one for a professional matchmaker?

Don't fall in love with your client.

I screwed that up when I fell for my best friend, Reid Fortino. He's gorgeous, successful, and sexy as hell. I figured it would be easy to find him a match—and save the family business at the same time.

But the more time I spend attempting to find the perfect girl, the more I realize how much I want him for my own. What's the harm if we give in for just one night?

I should have known that would never be enough.

Now I'm on the verge of losing my job and my heart.

We were an imperfect match from the start, but I don't know how to let him go.

Willow

"I'm retiring," my mother says as I sit in the chair across from her. "And I'm thinking of selling the business."

"You're what?" I stare over the desk at her in complete shock. "Mom, you can't be serious."

"It's time, Willow. Your dad and I want to travel the world while we still have the energy to do it."

"Okay, fine, but don't sell the business! My Heart's Desire is the number one matchmaking service in Chicago! You've spent twenty years of your life building it up." My mother is brilliant and has this innate ability to see a couple's potential without any explanation. It's like she sees through all the pretenses and lies, and gets to the heart of what a person really needs.

She sighs. "I know, darling, but I'm not getting any younger, and you're not getting any better at this."

It's the truth, but I feel like I have to defend myself anyway. "I'm still in training."

"Willow, it's been three years."

"It takes *time* to make a perfect match!"

"I had five marriages under my belt in my first year."

"Well … I've come close a few times, haven't I?" I don't actually know if this is true, but I like to think it is. I've set up countless clients, followed all of my mother's directions. I've agonized over finding the subtle nuances in interviews that I think a client would appreciate … but all my matches have been total busts.

I'm clearly a love disaster where my mother is a guru—in work and in life.

"I suppose I could ask Aspen to take it over," she muses, looking out the window.

"Aspen!" My jaw drops. My mother cannot truly think this is a good idea. I love my sister, but she needs psychiatric help … or even just a shower and haircut. She took my parents' hippie mentality and decided it was a life choice, much like being vegan or keto. She feels that she can't partake in anything that supports the government. Therefore, she lives on my parents' land, steals—or borrows, if you ask her—their electricity, water, food, and anything else she needs. Then tries to say she's "living off the land." I called it being a lazy ass.

And then a month ago, my mother hired her at My Heart's Desire as an administrative assistant. In that short time, she's already made two matches!

"Well, if I'm not going to sell it, I need someone to take over. Aspen is so new at this—I was hoping it would be you. In fact, that was the entire point of you coming to work for me. With your business degree, plus my mentoring, I figured it wouldn't take long for you to be ready, but ..." She gives me a pointed look as she trails off.

I sit up taller. "I am ready, Mom. Give me one more chance. I know I can find someone a perfect match."

She releases another heavy sigh. "And you know, I can't help but wish that out of all the people for whom I've found a soul mate, one of them could be you. I regret not finding *your* happily ever after. I'm positive that's your problem."

Here we go.

The fact that I'd rather be single than settle is a mystery to her. "It's not a problem, Mom. I'm happy. I don't currently need or want a man."

"You can lie to yourself, but not to me."

It's actually the truth. It's not that I don't believe in love, but I haven't been able to find it, and yet I'm very happy in my life. I live in a great apartment, I have the best across-the-hall neighbor ever (who also happens to be my best friend), I have plants to take care of, and no need whatsoever for another asshole boyfriend.

If there's a hole in my world, it's children. I grew up in the most insane, ridiculous home that ever existed, but I loved my childhood. We owned a beautiful lot up in Michigan with a freaking petting zoo. It was a time filled with new animals and trips out to the woods to search for buried treasure that my father hid the night before. It was sleeping under the stars, swimming in the lake, listening to ghost stories. (Later, it was my sister smoking plants that I'm sure my mother didn't know she was growing.)

I've always dreamed of children, marriage, and the picture-perfect happily ever after, with a little chaos thrown in.

The problem?

I have the worst taste in men *ever*. I'll think a guy is great, enjoy the first date, and then he asks for anal or something ridiculous on the second date and ... boom, single again. Yet another example of how much I suck at matchmaking ... I can't even find myself someone worthy of a second date.

But I've got a plan to get where I want to be. And while it doesn't require a husband, it *will* require me to have a job and an income. Seeing as I don't have another option lined up, I need to salvage this situation.

I try to redirect. "We're not talking about me, Mom. We're talking about the company."

"Fine, but is it too much to ask for a grandbaby before I'm in a wheelchair?"

"Mom, I'm thirty-two! You act like you're dying and I've failed to give you hope. Plus, we both know that Aspen will probably end up pregnant before me. Lord only knows what the hell goes on in that ridiculous Airstream she lives in."

My mother smiles wistfully. "Aspen is an old soul."

"And a hot mess," I grumble.

She mimics my words from a moment ago. "We're

not talking about your sister, we're talking about you, my Weeping Willow. You could find love, but you have no prospects because you spend all your time with Reid."

My mother both loves and hates my best friend.

"I do not spend all my time with Reid."

"Really? Who were you with last weekend?"

"Reid and I had plans," I say with indignation. I don't know why that's a big deal. He needed help, and I wasn't busy.

"Okay, and what about Monday night? What did you do?"

I hate where this is going. "I was at home."

"Alone?"

"No."

She smiles with fake sweetness. "Who were you with?"

"I was watching television ... with Reid." I tack the last part on softly.

"And the rest of the week? Did you have plans with friends?"

"I did, actually." Reid is a friend, so technically I'm not lying, right?

"Uh huh, and was the friend Reid?"

Damn her. "Yes, Mother. It was."

"And last night, were you busy with someone *other* than Reid?"

I glare at her because she knows damn well I was

watching TV with Reid because that's what we do every Thursday. It's our thing.

"So to recap, you spent last weekend, Monday, Tuesday, Wednesday, and Thursday with him?"

My mother is a pain in my ass. A big one.

"Willow?" she nudges.

I roll my eyes. "Yes, okay? Yes, I spent all those evenings with Reid!"

"Did someone say my name?"

Speak of the devil and all that ...

I groan and look back to see Reid Fortino himself standing in the doorway, looking like he owns the place. His dark brown hair is pushed to the side and he's wearing a very expensive black suit with a crisp blue shirt underneath, which makes his eyes appear even bluer. Broad shoulders with thick arms and a tapered waist make most women get all tongue-tied around him.

I like to tease him about looking like the male version of Xena the Warrior Princess—dark and brooding with that hint of danger ... you're not sure if you want to run from him or maul him. Even though I have zero romantic feelings for Reid, I can't deny how hot he is. He had a meeting today in the building and said if he finished early, he would stop by. I didn't realize what time it was.

Normally, I'd be happy to see him, but he always enjoys when my mother picks on me about my relationship status, and he loves to argue with her.

I look at the ceiling. "Really, God? Really? You couldn't have dropped anyone else at the door? It had to be him?"

"Which only proves my point," Mom gloats.

"What's up, Wills?" Reid asks, entering the office. "Were you talking about me or something?"

I straighten my head and look at him. "Yes, my mother was just saying that you're killing my love life."

He smirks. "I'm saving her, Mrs. Hayes. That's all. I keep the dirtbags away and—"

"And you keep the worthy ones from approaching," she says in her chastising-mother voice.

"You wound me." Reid clutches his chest.

Mom laughs with a shake of her head and I watch him charm her into submission. It's amazing and kind of scary to watch women around him. He's smooth, good looking, and has an ability to make even smart, strong women do his bidding. Well, all except me.

I'm completely immune to his charm, or as I call it, his bullshit.

"I doubt that very much, honey," my mother tells him. "If you're going to keep Willow from finding love, the least you could do is date her."

He nearly chokes and I burst out laughing. This might actually be fun for once. "He won't date me, Mom. He doesn't find me attractive."

"I never said—" Reid starts before getting interrupted.

"You don't think she's pretty?" Mom asks, as though he's a crazy person.

"I think she's beautiful." Reid looks to me for help.

Instead of bailing him out of what will surely be a painful conversation with my mother, I lean back in my chair with a shit-eating grin. *You're on your own, buddy.*

"Then why is the idea of dating her so terrible?" Mom presses.

"It's not." Reid loosens his tie.

"So you just want to monopolize her time but not allow her to find love?"

He opens his mouth, shaking his head but my mother is already on to her next question.

"You don't think she's worthy of finding love?"

"I didn't—"

"And what about the guys she does date, do you think it's okay to scare them off by walking around her apartment as though you live there?"

I nod. "Right, so unfair."

Reid glares at me with open hostility. Which makes me grin wider.

My mother folds her arms over her chest. "If you're not willing to date her, then you should at least allow her the opportunity to find someone else."

Reid struggles briefly for a reply, and then smiles like he's got it all figured out. "I know, Mrs. Hayes, but it's hard because Willow chases away the girls I bring home too."

Oh, that bastard.

He's so full of shit. First, he thinks what my mother does is total bullshit. Second, he doesn't even date; he just sleeps with random bar girls and *calls* it dating. All he's doing is deflecting now, and when my mother turns to look at me, I can see it worked.

Damn it.

"Willow!"

He smiles triumphantly at me, and now it's my turn to glare. "I don't do that, Mom. I've tried to find him a nice girl, but he rejects them all."

My mother's gaze shifts back to him and I stick my tongue out at him, like the mature adult I am.

"It's just not true, Mrs. Hayes," Reid protests. "I *have* tried to find someone, but Wills is the reason all the girls say they can't love me. And I can't choose some stranger over my best friend. You understand, don't you?"

My mouth falls open because he just played her like a fiddle. My mother will never be able to resist his little wounded boy sob story. There's nothing she likes more than someone she can fix.

Drat.

"Oh, honey, I didn't know." She gets to her feet and pulls him into her arms.

Reid looks over her shoulder at me like the cat that ate the canary. "I've really struggled with this. You know, emotionally. I'm very sensitive that way."

For the love of God.

I flip him off as he tries to stifle his laughter. It almost looks like he's shaking with tears.

"Mom! You can't believe him, he's full of shit!"

Her arms drop and the disappointment in her eyes towards me only fuels my fire. "Willow Hayes, this man just showed a true bout of heartsickness over his desire to find love, and you chastise him?"

"You seriously don't believe that, do you?"

Reid covers his face with his hands.

"Oh, Reid." My mother says his name with a gasp. "I'm so sorry, honey."

And then he's fake-weeping in her arms again.

I'm going to kill him tonight. But how? I'm thinking food poisoning, since I've never known him to turn anything edible away. It would definitely be the easiest option and the least messy. Shooting him seems too bloody. And he's way too strong for me to choke, although the way he's grinning at me again might give me Herculean strength.

I move my mouth but don't make a sound. *I'm going to kill you.*

He smiles wider and mouths back, *I'd like to see you try.*

Game on, jackass.

Reid

Willow's mother rocks me in her arms like the sad, pathetic, unloved man I'm pretending to be. All the while, I'm looking at Wills and trying not to laugh.

She and I both know my act is total crap.

I'm not unloved or sad. She might say my inability to cook and shop for myself is pathetic, but as I remind her, she *enjoys* doing those things for me. I wouldn't want to take that away from her.

The truth is, I'm a normal guy with the best friend in the world living across the hall. She makes sure I'm fed, and she ensures I don't look like a total loser by helping me pick out clothes. More than that, she's always there for me.

When my dog died, Willow was there.

When my idiot brother Leo moved in because his girlfriend kicked him out, Willow helped make sure I didn't kill him.

When my ex-girlfriend cheated on me, Willow was the one offering to help bury the body. (Glinda was not the good witch she pretended to be.)

There's nothing in this world I treasure more than our friendship.

Nothing.

Right now though, if looks could kill, she'd have murdered me six ways till Sunday.

"Come sit." Mrs. Hayes pulls me toward the chair.

Not wanting to let this charade die, I sniff as though I'm holding back tears.

Which earns me a major eye roll from Wills. "Oh, please," she says under her breath.

"I want you two to have someone in your lives to share more than just pizza and Chinese food with. You need a real relationship," Mrs. Hayes says while glancing back and forth between us. "I know you're friends, and it's so important to have that platonic affection too, but you need someone to love romantically who will love you back the same way." Before either of us can say anything, she lifts her hands. "Not that you two don't love each other, but you don't *love* love each other. I think we can all agree on that."

Willow sighs and nods, and she and I exchange a look.

No one gets our friendship. She's beautiful, not to mention funny, smart, and put together in that I'm-a-Real-Adult way, but it's never been romantic for us.

We've somehow managed to keep our friendship securely in the friend zone.

"My point is that maybe you guys are hurting each other instead of helping," her mother goes on.

"Mom, we're fine." Willow holds up her hands. "We really are. Reid is happy. I'm happy. Not everyone needs to be married to be happy."

Her mother turns to me with her best maternal stare. "Do you want a wife and children?"

The truth is no, I don't. I don't want any part of being a dad, or a husband, or turning into any version of my own father. I grew up with the most fucked-up parents a person could have. Mom is a raging alcoholic. Dad works constantly to avoid my drunk mom, and my brother and I had to fend for ourselves more often than not. They had all the money in the world, but they were miserable, and they made us miserable too. Why would I want to repeat that?

But I don't want to get into my fucked-up family history with Mrs. Hayes. I've barely talked to Willow about it. I prefer to leave it in the past where it belongs.

"I'm not sure I want a wife and kids," I say hesitantly, deciding to tack on another lie to avoid follow-up questions. "At least, not right now. Maybe in the distant future, if I met the right person."

Then she turns to Willow. "And you?"

"You know I want kids. Sooner rather than later."

"Then why don't you help each other? Or at least stop sabotaging each other?"

"What do you mean?" I ask.

"Let Willow try to find you a match, Reid."

"What?" My voice cracks in horror.

"We *are* a matchmaking service."

"Yes, but ..."

Willow clears her throat. "Mom, you can't think this is a good—"

She continues on like neither of us protested. "Willow needs the chance to prove herself here, and you, Reid Fortino, need someone who loves you enough to find you the perfect girl. What do you say?"

"Um ..." I unbutton my collar, which suddenly feels too tight around my throat. "I'm not really—"

"I mean, neither of you is getting any younger," Mrs. Hayes points out, prompting Willow and I to exchange an eye roll. "I know women don't like to hear this, but there is a fertility window."

"*Mom*. Can we not discuss this right now?"

"Why not? It's a biological fact."

"I get it, and I already have a plan in place. You know that. In fact," she says, taking a breath, "I have an appointment at the clinic to discuss options."

My skin crawls. My hands curl into fists. If she wants kids, then great, I want that for her, but if she talks about artificial whatever-the-hell-it's-called one more time, I might puke. The thought of some weird asshole's *stuff* inside her makes me sick. What kind of pervy losers are jerking off in those clinics anyway?

"I support that plan, darling, but that doesn't help

Reid with his co-dependency issues," her mother says. "He needs a match to cure his loneliness. And *you* need a romantic success story under your belt to give you the confidence you need to take this business to the next level, so *I* can sit on a beach in St. Croix and wait for news of the impending birth of my grandbaby." Mrs. Hayes beams beatifically, as if it all makes perfect sense.

I need to speak up, like right the fuck now. "Listen, Mrs. Hayes, I appreciate your concern for my loneliness, but there's no way in hell Willow is going to be able to find me a match. No sense getting her hopes up."

Willow sits up straighter in her chair and arches a brow at me. "And just what do you mean by that?"

"I mean that you're not going to be able to turn me into a romantic success story, Wills. And I don't want you to be disappointed."

Mrs. Hayes sucks in a breath and puts a hand over her heart. "I'm surprised at you, Reid Fortino. Willow needs us to believe in her. Are you saying she isn't good at her job?"

Damn. The woman is good. "No! I do believe in her. I just—"

"I'll do it." Willow stands up and gives me a defiant look. "I'll take you on." Then she aims the look at her mother. "And I'll prove to you that I *can* take over the business."

I raise my eyebrows. I can't tell if this is a joke, if I pissed her off too much and she's trying to get back at me, or if she honestly thinks she's going to be able to find my soul mate, as if such a thing exists.

"Wonderful." Mrs. Hayes clasps her hands at her chest. "Now let's have a group hug."

Willow comes over to us with a glint in her eye and the two of them hug me from opposite sides, while I stand there feeling like a piece of wood in a vise.

What the hell just happened?

❄

"Are you crazy?" I ask Willow as I pull open the door of a cab. "Why would you tell your mother you can find me a match?"

"Mostly because you said it couldn't be done." She gives me a grin as she slides across the back seat. "I can't resist a chance to prove you wrong. It's too much fun. Plus you deserved it for feeding her that crap about how I chase away the girls you bring home. As if you give a shit about any of them."

Groaning, I get in next to her and shut the door. "This is not going to end well for you."

"Maybe, maybe not."

I give the driver the address of our building and sit back, giving Willow a pained look. "You've told me a million times that you're terrible at this. That your mom only hired you because her previous assistant quit unexpectedly and you'd just gotten fired."

"I didn't get fired, asshole," she says huffily, poking me in the leg. "I was let go because I refused to massage the data like the V.P wanted me to. I lost my job because I was honest."

"I know, I'm just giving you a hard time." Honestly, I'm glad she doesn't work for that finance company anymore. I met that dickhead V.P. a few times, and I'm positive the data wasn't the only thing he wanted her to massage. "You know I think you could be great at anything, including this romantic shit. I just don't need or want it."

"Methinks you doth protest too much, my friend. Maybe my mother is right about you, and behind all those walls you put up beats a heart that's longing to find its mate." She links her fingers beneath her chin and leans toward me, batting her lashes.

I put my hand over her face and push her away. "Quit it, you lunatic. You don't believe in that stuff any more than I do."

She laughs and straightens up. "It's not that I don't believe in it. I just don't have good romantic luck myself because all the guys I've dated have turned out to be dipshits."

"You can say that again," I mutter. Willow's taste in guys is beyond horrible.

"But this isn't about me. It's about you. And I know you well enough to find you the perfect girl." She nods slowly. "You know, the more I think about it, this is totally win-win for me. I prove myself to my mother and I get to have complete control over who you date for the next six months."

"Six months?" I gape at her.

"Duh, it takes time to find perfection," she says, like I'm a first grader. Then she toughens up her tone, pointing a finger at me. "And you better play nice. No fair sabotaging these dates or refusing to go."

I groan as my life starts to pass me by in a haze of terrible dates with desperate girls who have what my brother Leo calls an FFR—Face For Radio. "And what do I get in return for going through with this ridiculousness?"

"Everlasting love, of course." She flicks my shoulder.

"Not good enough. I want something from you."

"Like what?"

I think for a moment. "If I take this seriously, you have to promise me you're not going to let some jerk-off from the spank bank knock you up."

She sighs heavily and rolls her eyes. "One has nothing to do with the other, Reid."

"Doesn't matter. I think you're rushing into it and I want you to reconsider. I can't believe you didn't tell me you made an appointment." The cab pulls up in front of our building, and I swipe my card in the reader.

"I didn't tell you because I knew you'd throw a tantrum about it," she says as we get out of the car. "You've been weird ever since I told you about my plan."

I shut the door behind her. "It's the plan that's weird, not me. How can you think this is a good idea? You're completely rational about every other thing in life." We walk together toward the entrance, and I pull open the heavy glass door to the lobby.

"This is absolutely a rational, not an emotional, decision," she says, giving me a pointed look over her shoulder. "*You're* the one getting emotional about it."

I try to think up an argument as we head for the elevators, but I can't. "You know that stuff about a window is bullshit," I finally say as she punches the up button. "Women are having babies later and later in life."

"It's not bullshit, actually. Age thirty-five is considered advanced maternal age, and a lot of women are having to resort to expensive fertility treatments to get pregnant. IVF with egg donors and all that. An IUI is a much more budget-friendly way to go." The elevator doors open, and after a few people exit, we step in.

The doors close and I turn to her. "What the fuck's an IUI?"

"An intrauterine insemination. It's the thing I told you about before."

"Where they let some creep who wanked into a cup knock you up with a turkey baster?"

She rolls her eyes. "Don't be so dramatic."

"I'm serious, Wills. You think Olympic athletes and rocket scientists are in there flogging the dolphin? Use your head. It's deadbeats and weirdos. Why am I the only one who cares about your baby's genetic makeup?"

The elevator dings at our floor and the door opens. "Fine, Reid. You agree to go at this match thing with an open mind, and I will put off my appointment at the fertility clinic."

"*And* rethink that plan," I add as we walk down the hall toward our apartments. "I can't even believe your mother is okay with it."

"My mother wants grandkids, and it's as clear to her as it is to me that it's not going to happen the usual way." She pulls her keys from her bag. "Why can't you just support me?"

"I can. I do. I just …" How can I explain it to her without sounding like a possessive asshole? I'm not even sure why I hate the idea so much. I love Willow and I want her to be happy. If having a baby on her own will make her happy, why can't I just shut up and support her? We reach our doors, and I grab her arm before she puts her key in the lock. "Look, I'm sorry. But you know I can't keep my mouth shut when I have something to say, especially when it pertains to you."

She snorts. "True story."

"So do we have a deal? I go on some dates with whoever you choose and you hold off on the intergalactic insemination?"

A smile tugs her lips. "Intra*uterine* insemination."

"Whatever."

"Yes, we have a deal. But while you and the future Mrs. Fortino are planning your wedding, I will be moving forward at the fertility clinic, and I'll expect your full support."

My stomach heaves, but I hold out my hand and we shake on it.

Although there is no way in hell I am letting any of that shit go down.

Willow

He shook on it!

I sort of can't believe it. Reid can be mouthy and obnoxious and way too cocky for his own good, but I've never known him to break a promise or renege on a deal. Success—and a brand new purpose in life—would be mine.

All I have to do is find Reid a match.

"Hey, what are you doing later? You want to come over and watch Netflix or something? Get some food?" I ask him as I'm unlocking my door. The more time I can spend secretly probing his brain, the closer I'll be able to get to his ideal woman.

"Sure. I don't have any plans tonight."

I grin at him over my shoulder. "There's a shock."

He pokes me in the ribs. "Like your dance card is so full these days? When's the last time you even went on a date?"

"Why should I bother with dates when I have vodka and This Is Us right here at home? My night would end exactly the same, but this way I can cry on my couch without having to put on my skinny jeans first."

He shakes his head. "I am not watching any more of that show."

"Then I'm not feeding you. And you'll be sad because I'm making one of your favorites."

His eyes light up. "The ziti?"

"The ziti," I confirm.

"Damn." He frowns, and I can see him weighing a giant plateful of baked ziti against suffering through my favorite Friday night show. "Okay, fine. I'll come."

I give him a satisfied smile and opened my door. "I knew you would. Come over in an hour."

Scowling like a little boy, he grumbles something I don't catch, and I shut the door in his face.

I'm still smiling after I've changed out of my work clothes into plaid flannel pants and a big, sloppy gray sweatshirt. Nothing better than getting out of heels and a bra at the end of the day. I toss my hair into a messy bun and head for the kitchen, where I put the ziti together.

While I work, I put MSNBC on my iPad, which is propped on my cookbook easel, but I don't really pay attention to the news. I'm carefully cataloging everything I know about Reid Fortino, and trying to see him in a different light. A romantic light.

He's gorgeous—no denying that—and with my help, he's learned to dress better. I'll have to style him for his dates, but that's not a problem. He's got a great sense of humor (although he likes to make fun of me too much), so I definitely need to find him a girl who likes to laugh. He works quite a bit, but he's moving up the ladder at a trendy new marketing and PR firm, so she has to be understanding of his crazy work schedule. She'll also have to put up with the occasional client dinner—I've done a few of these when Reid needed a date on short notice with no expectations—but they aren't terrible. And it's kind of fun to watch Reid turn on the charm and go all "ad man" on prospective clients. He really is creative, persuasive, and smart.

As I layer the cooked pasta and meaty sauce into the baking dish, I consider his faults—the things any woman who's really looking for love is going to notice sooner or later.

First, he doesn't trust women. It's because he was burned so badly in the past. His parents are a train wreck, the absolute worst example of a marriage. And then, he thought maybe he could make it with his ex and ended up getting burned, which I get, but he's really got to put that behind him.

Second, he often doesn't think before he speaks, and it can get him into a shitload of trouble. Pair that with his healthy Italian temper, and you've got a recipe for disaster. Not that he has anger issues, but damn—his emotions run hot and close to the surface, and if you really say something to piss him off, watch out.

His favorite thing in the world to do is eat, so she's got to be a good cook, or at least willing to learn, because while he will happily make the drinks and do the dishes, he is beyond clueless in the kitchen.

There's only one thing about him that really baffles me. His love of comics. Not just comic books, though, but the entire world. I don't understand it. He goes to all those conventions, dresses in full costumes, and ... I can't even. But he's never happier than when he puts on some weird getup to go play with lightsabers in a tournament. He also knows it makes me roll my eyes so hard they hurt, which means he drags me to them at every opportunity.

Hence, three days a week I find the sappiest drama-ridden shows I can find and force him to sit and suffer through them.

But I suppose the biggest problem with finding him a match is that he's really fucking picky when it comes to women. I've suggested he take out a couple different friends of mine, but he always finds something wrong with them—either they're too shy or they won't shut up or they're just not his type. I'll have to dig deep tonight and figure out what that type really is.

I stick the ziti in the oven and set the timer for fifty-five minutes. After that, I straighten up my living room, water my plants, and throw in a load of laundry. I'm in the kitchen putting together a salad when Reid knocks three times and opens the door without my answering it.

"I brought you a present," he says, joining me in the kitchen. He sets a brown paper bag on the counter and pulls out a bottle of Tito's and a jar of fancy olives.

"Thanks!" I give him a big grin and pat his bicep. "But you still have to watch my show."

He groans. "If it didn't smell so good in here, I'd leave." Going over to the oven, he opens it and peeks in. "Mother of God, that looks amazing."

"When we find your future wife, I'll give her the recipe."

"Looks like you're going to be cooking for me the rest of our lives."

"Oh, ye of little faith." I'm going to find him a wife, if it's the last damn thing I do. He thought he was so funny today, but I'll get the last laugh. I get in his face and point a finger at him. "I bet you'll be married within a year."

"You're really cute when you're determined."

"Flattery will get you nowhere, my friend."

He laughs, grabs the jar of Tito's and my cocktail shaker. "You know, you were my favorite person in the world before today, when you sided with your mother on getting my wagon hitched."

"I'll be your favorite again when you're eating the ziti," I toss back.

"This is true."

He's so predictable. This is another thing I'll have to watch for. Reid is smart and he likes women who can keep up with his wit and sarcasm. Not only will she need to be pretty, but she has to challenge him.

I don't want to show it, but the task is starting to feel a bit daunting. Reid can be a pain in the ass, and finding someone to love him and put up with his shit is part one, but then finding someone *he* will put up with might prove impossible.

My mother is really evil for suggesting the idea.

"Do you want it dirty or straight up?" Reid asks.

"Dirty, please."

A few minutes later, he hands me a drink that's the perfect mix of vodka, dry vermouth, and olive juice, with four olives instead of the customary two, and I smile. "You're the best."

"I know."

"And so humble."

"I call it honest." Reid's smirk makes me want to slap him.

We both sit at the table, waiting for the food to cook, and I figure this is the best chance to talk about the whole matchmaking thing. I have a limited amount of time to find his dream girl and get them to fall in love. It occurs to me I might lose my best friend in the process, which makes me sad. I let out a heavy sigh, and run my finger around the stem of the glass.

"What's that face?" he asks. "Something wrong?"

I hate that he can read me so damn well. But I don't tell him what I'm really thinking. "Nope. Just thinking of what I can ask you so I'm sure to find that perfect girl."

"Oh, Jesus. Well, ask your questions already, so we can get this over with and I can eat in peace."

"And then watch an hour of beautiful storytelling in the most heartbreaking way."

He groans. "I regret this already."

"As you should."

I spend the next thirty minutes grilling him and enjoying every second of his torture.

❄

The next day at work, I sit at my desk, sifting through the potential matches for Reid from the database of eligible females.

There's something wrong with *all* of them.

"Hmm, too tall."

"Too stupid."

"Too ... blond."

I sigh and drop my face into my hands. I've been at this for four hours and I only have one maybe on the pile. He is seriously proving to be impossible to match. It doesn't help that the list of requisite traits he came up with last night was asinine. There is no way any girl will have a check in every box, but I have to at least find the majority checked or he'll toss her before she gets a chance.

Stupid, stubborn man.

I'm going to find another tearjerker show to torment him with because of all the grief this is putting me through.

"How's it going?" Mom asks.

I look up from the list with more red X's on it than circles, with a face that clearly says how much fun I'm not having.

"That good, I see."

"You couldn't have picked anyone else? Anyone? You had to assign me the man who has no desire to get married? All these women want to date someone who might actually propose someday. That's never gonna be Reid."

She smiles with that motherly look she's perfected and shrugs. "Life is full of challenges and I don't think Reid knows what he wants. He will when he finds her. You just have to bring her to him, which is what we do, Willow. We force people to open their horizons to ideas they don't think they believe in. Most of my clients couldn't find the right person not because they didn't want love, but because they weren't willing to truly open their eyes."

"Right, but Reid didn't come to us. You forced him on me."

"I gave him the option, and he walked through that door. He's ready for love, he's just afraid to take the risk."

"And you think I'm going to be able to show him the light?"

Mom smiles and nods. "I know you will. He'll see it."

My mother lives in a universe of eternal optimism. It's exhausting most days, but then, she's usually right, which makes it hard to argue with her. "Well, I need options and we are short on those."

"I have all the faith in the world that there's someone in our database for him."

"I'm glad one of us does," I mutter under my breath. "I'm leaving here in about five minutes. Reid and I are going to get him a few new outfits and then he's forcing me to go to the comic store."

"Life is all about compromise, darling."

"Like you do with Dad?"

She laughs through her nose. "No honey, that's twenty-plus years of marriage and knowing when to smile and nod. Men like to *think* they're important and have a say, when we all know the women are truly in charge."

"Good advice."

"I give it to all my clients after their weddings. Just like you can to Reid and his bride once you succeed."

Right. "Well, on that note. I should get going." I grab my purse and kiss my mother on the cheek.

"Have fun!" she calls as I walk out.

"Yeah, nothing says fun like the comic store!" I say as the door closes behind me.

On the elevator down, I shoot him a quick text reminding him that we're going shopping. He has stood me up one too many times for my liking.

> Meet me outside the store.

REID
> What store?

Oh my God. I knew it.

> Reid! We have a shopping date.

REID
> Who is this? I don't know this number.

I'm going to kill him.

> Funny. I'll see you in ten.

REID
> Seriously, stalking is a punishable crime. I request that you find another man for your attention.

> You realize I know where you live. Also, I feed you, and nothing says revenge like Ex-Lax.

REID
> Touché, my evil friend.

I huff and put my AirPods in as I stroll down the Chicago streets. It's so nice out today. It's beautiful for October, and I couldn't be happier. I have a cute fall sweater on, and with the sun, it feels at least ten degrees warmer than it probably is.

I think about each female face I pass on the sidewalk in a different way, wondering if she could be the one for him. I catalog their features, whether they smile as I pass, their height, weight, and overall stature. I keep hoping for lightning to strike, to find *that* girl. The one that will change his mind about marriage, open his eyes and his horizons, like my mother said. She has faith, so why shouldn't I?

Then Reid can get hitched, and I can get pregnant.

However, with each girl I study, I find something wrong. I start to question myself, and I wonder if I was being too hard on all the women in the database.

Why aren't they good enough to even show him? Why am I being so damn picky on his behalf? Maybe he'd like the tall girl. Maybe he will date someone who can't spell. Maybe I'm not giving him enough credit.

Before I can come to any conclusions, I plow into someone and nearly go over backward. "Shit! Sorry."

Reid's blue eyes meet mine as he catches me, and then his grin widens. "Wills. I always knew you'd try to fall at my feet."

"Yeah, that's it."

"You okay?" His hands are gripping my shoulders,

keeping me from falling over, and I nod, straightening up.

"Yeah, I was in my head."

"Scary place that is."

"Not as scary as I was going to be if you didn't show."

He shakes his head and opens the large glass door of the department store. "After you, my lady."

"Thank you, kind sir." Delighted with his manners, I touch his arm as I walk past him and then he slaps me on the ass.

I give him a dirty look over my shoulder. "And they say chivalry is dead."

"That was for the Ex-Lax comment. Never threaten my food again."

I flip him off and decide to exact my revenge in other ways. After all, I control his dates for the next six months.

After an hour of Reid complaining as I pick out new clothes that don't consist of Spiderman T-shirts and track pants, we're finally done. I swear, he's the most difficult human on the planet some days.

We found some nice formal and casual clothes. The kind of first-impression outfits that women appreciate. No one wants to date a slob, which he's really not. He's just a little juvenile sometimes. I find it endearing and funny, but other girls might not.

"What are we doing tonight?" he asks as we walk out.

"Well, I'm working. I have to find your next hot date."

He groans under his breath. "Why do you hate me?"

"Because you'll need company when I have my baby—"

"Not by some douchebag with a turkey baster."

I huff. "When it happens, and I'm a mom, things will change for us. I don't hate you, I just want you to be happy too."

Reid starts to loosen his tie, which I know is a telltale sign that he's uncomfortable and doesn't want to talk about this, but maybe my mother was right. Maybe the two of us keep holding the other back because we're comfortable.

He's a great guy. He's everything that most women want, except maybe for the fact that he can't boil water and isn't very willing to share the remote, and yet he's alone. I know Glinda was a bitch in the end, but that was years ago. Since then, he's been dating the dumbest girls he can find so there's no danger of entering a real relationship, and the rest of his time he spends with me.

Lord knows I never want to admit my mother could be right, but ... I can see it.

"Things *will* change, Reid. We're both going to have to realize that and maybe it's time we grow up."

"I think we're pretty fucking grown up. And you

and I both know I don't want a wife. I refuse to be my fucking father."

I bite my lip. It's so hard to watch him beat himself up over someone that he's *nothing* like. His father is cold and distant. Reid is warm and sweet. He cares about his family. He took his brother Leo in with no questions asked. I wish he wouldn't be so rough on himself.

"One day you're going to wake up and realize that you and Vince Fortino are not the same person."

"His blood is still mine."

I touch his arm, squeezing gently. "Reid, that may be true, but your heart is nothing like his."

"Glinda didn't think so."

Don't even get me started on that bitch. "She was an idiot. She's still an idiot, wherever she is."

He smiles and I see him trying to hide the hurt that lies under it all. "Maybe, but I can't fuck up a marriage like he did if I don't enter one."

"I've never known you to shy away from a risk."

"This isn't a risk, Willow. It's guaranteed failure. I'm not cut out for it. And why are you so anxious to get rid of me, all of a sudden?" He elbows me in the ribs.

"I'm not," I protest.

"Well, good. Because I like how things are. I don't want them to change. Do you?"

I'm not sure how to answer. In a way, I don't want things to change either. I've always known that if either of us finds *the one*, what we have will be gone. But thinking it could happen sooner rather than later is a little sad, even if it does mean reaching my goal of becoming a mom.

Because I love my time with Reid. I love our easy friendship and the way we have no expectations or demands. He is truly my best friend and if he gets married, he'll belong to someone else. And the baby I'm going to have will be my priority, instead of him.

But life has to move forward, doesn't it?

"Yes, Reid. I do want things to change," I admit. "I want to start the next phase of my life, raise a child, and have ... something."

He stops walking and looks at me. "You do have something. You have us."

I look up into his blue eyes and touch his chest. "I have us. I know. You're my best friend, and I love you. Always will. And I want you by my side through everything. But ..."

"But you want a Butterball."

"What?"

"A turkey-baster baby."

I sigh heavily. "This is why we can't ever have a serious conversation. You're an infant."

He pulls me close. "See? You don't need a kid, you got me."

I groan and bang my head against his chest, wishing I could magically transport to a place where men weren't so stupid.

Reid doesn't have to understand it, I just need him to support me. Hopefully, once I find him the love of his life, he won't give a crap about my baby-making parts.

This will be a win-win.

Won't it?

Also by Melanie Harlow and Corinne Michaels

Co-Written Novels by Melanie Harlow and Corinne Michaels

Hold You Close

Imperfect Match

Books by Corinne Michaels

The Salvation Series

Beloved

Beholden

Consolation

Conviction

Defenseless

Evermore: A 1001 Dark Night Novella

Indefinite

Infinite

The Hennington Brothers

Say You'll Stay

Say You Want Me

Say I'm Yours

Say You Won't Let Go: A Return to Me/Masters and Mercenaries Novella

Second Time Around Series

We Own Tonight

One Last Time

Not Until You

If I Only Knew

The Arrowood Brothers

Come Back for Me

Fight for Me

The One for Me

Stay for Me

Destined for Me: An Arrowood/Hennington Brothers Crossover Novella

Willow Creek Valley Series

Return to Us

Could Have Been Us

A Moment for Us

A Chance for Us

Rose Canyon Series

Help Me Remember

Give Me Love

Keep This Promise

Sugarloaf Series (Coming 2023-2024)

Forbidden Hearts

Broken Dreams

Tempting Promises

Forgotten Desires

Standalone Novels

All I Ask

You Loved Me Once

Want a downloadable reading order?

https://geni.us/CM_ReadingGuide

Books by Melanie Harlow

The Frenched Series

Frenched

Yanked

Forked

Floored

The Happy Crazy Love Series

Some Sort of Happy

Some Sort of Crazy

Some Sort of Love

The After We Fall Series

Man Candy

After We Fall

If You Were Mine

From This Moment

The One and Only Series

Only You

Only Him

Only Love

The Cloverleigh Farms Series

Irresistible

Undeniable

Insatiable

Unbreakable

Unforgettable

The Bellamy Creek Series

Drive Me Wild

Make Me Yours

Call Me Crazy

Tie Me Down

Cloverleigh Farms Next Generation Series

Ignite

Taste

Tease

Tempt

Co-Written Books

Strong Enough (M/M romance co-written with David Romanov)

The Speak Easy Duet

The Tango Lesson (A Standalone Novella)

Want a reading order?

http://www.melanieharlow.com/reading-order/

About the Authors

Corinne Michaels is a *New York Times*, *USA Today*, and *Wall Street Journal* bestselling author of romance novels. Her stories are chock full of emotion, humor, and unrelenting love, and she enjoys putting her characters through intense heartbreak before finding a way to heal them through their struggles.

Corinne is a former Navy wife and happily married to the man of her dreams. She began her writing career after spending months away from her husband while he was deployed—reading and writing were her escapes from the loneliness. Corinne now lives in Virginia with her husband and is the emotional, witty, sarcastic, and fun-loving mom of two beautiful children.

Connect with Corinne:
Facebook: https://bit.ly/1iwLh6y

Instagram: https://bit.ly/2L1Vzo6
Goodreads: https://bit.ly/2N1H2Gb
Amazon: http://amzn.to/1NVZmhv
Bookbub: https://bit.ly/2yc6rss

Stay up to date with Corinne and sign up for her mailing list:
https://corinnemichaels.com/subscribe/

To sign up for monthly text alerts: Text CMBOOKS TO 77948
US only due to carrier restrictions

USA Today bestselling author Melanie Harlow likes her martinis dry, her heels high, and her history with the naughty bits left in. When she's not writing or reading, she gets her kicks from TV series like VEEP, Game of Thrones, and Homeland. She occasionally runs three miles, but only so she can have more gin and steak.

She lifts her glass to romance readers and writers from her home near Detroit, MI, where she lives with her husband, two daughters, and pet rabbit.

Connect with Melanie:
Facebook: https://bit.ly/1RiTP7z
Amazon: http://amzn.to/1NPkYKs
Bookbub: https://bit.ly/2yfljWR
Pinterest: https://bit.ly/2m60beu

Instagram: https://bit.ly/2ubxh19

Website: http://www.melanieharlow.com

Stay up to date with Melanie, sign up for her Mailing List: http://www.melanieharlow.com/subscribe/

Printed in Great Britain
by Amazon